Seder Order:

1 Blessing on the Wine — Kadesh קַדֵּשׁ

2 Wa… Yo…

3 Karpas כַּרְפַּס — Parsley in Salt Water

4 Yachatz יַחַץ — Making the Afikomen

5 Maggeed מַגִּיד — Telling the Passover Story

6 Rachatz רַחַץ — Washing Your Hands

7 מוֹצִיא מַצָּה Motzee Matzah — Eating Matzah

8 מָרוֹר Maror — Bitter Herbs

9 Koraych כּוֹרֵךְ — Sandwich

10 Shulchon Oraych שֻׁלְחָן עוֹרֵךְ — Festive Meal

11 Tzofun צָפוּן — The Afikomen

12 Baraych בָּרֵךְ — Grace After the Meal

13 Hallel הַלֵּל — Songs of Praise

14 Nirtzah נִרְצָה — Closing Prayer

ISRAEL

My Animated Haggadah and Story of Passover

Written and Illustrated by
Jacqueline Jacobson Pliskin

MAROR - BITTER HERBS
KARPAS - PARSLEY
CHAROSES - APPLE · NUTS · WINE
פסח
BAYTZA - ROASTED EGG
SHANK BONE - ZEROA
CHAZERET - LETTUCE
MATZAH

To my wonderful husband Jerry;
My beautiful daughters; Amy Lynn and Sheryl Elyse;
My loving parents, Lillian and Murray Jacobson, who taught me
the love of Judaism;
And my dearest in-laws, Herman and Rosalind Pliskin, who
taught me how to make chicken soup.

About the Author
and Illustrator
JACQUELINE JACOBSON PLISKIN

Jacqueline has written and illustrated "MY VERY OWN ANIMATED JEWISH HOLIDAY ACTIVITY BOOK," filled with stories, games and puzzles; and three popular children's books: "SOON I'LL BE... A Birthday Book for Boys and Girls," "THE ADVENTURES OF SIMCHA THE SEAL," and "SIMCHA THE SEAL SAVES THE SHATTERED SHABBAT," co-authored "THREE PLAYS FOR THE PRIMARY GRADES": designed and illustrated two educational series called "COLOR-A- SONG": and a Jewish holiday music activity coloring book "COLOR 'N' SING"; plus designed a series of Jewish puzzle and stationery designs.

She graduated from Brooklyn College, with degrees in art and education, attended the School of Visual Arts and painted at the Art Student's League. She has taught from pre-school to the college level and has served as an art director of a weekly newspaper and a monthly magazine.

Her other interests include painting, and theatre. In the last eight years, Jacqueline has won awards for several of her art works and paintings which she has exhibited extensively since her move to New Jersey in 1983. In addition, she directs a theatre group specializing in Jewish themes.

Jacqueline resides in East Brunswick, New Jersey, with her husband Jerry and her two teenage daughters, Amy Lynn and Sheryl Elyse.

A Shapolsky Book
Published by Shapolsky Publishers

Copyright © 1991 by Jacqueline Jacobson Pliskin
3rd Printing

For additional information, contact:
Shapolsky Publishers, Inc., 212-633-2022, 136 West 22nd Street, New York, N.Y. 10011

Getting Ready for the Seder

Seder means order. Haggadah means story. We use this Haggadah to read the story of Passover in the Passover service.

We help Mother get ready for the Seder. She prepares all the special foods after the house has been made ready. All chometz - leavened bread and food not allowed for Passover — has been cleaned away the day before.

Mother lights the candles on the holiday table.

After all the family and friends who will join us tonight are seated at the table, we start the Seder.

Blessing Over the Wine

Kadesh

קַדֵּשׁ

With the matzah covered, we hold up the wine and say the blessing.

"Blessed are You, Lord our God, King of the Universe, who creates the fruit of the vine."

"Baruch Atah Adonay Eloheynu Melech haolam boray peree hagafen."

בָּרוּךְ אַתָּה יְיָ, אֱלֹהֵינוּ מֶלֶךְ הָעוֹלָם, בּוֹרֵא פְּרִי הַגָּפֶן:

"Blessed are You, Lord our God, who has made Israel and the festivals holy."

"Baruch Atah Adonay mekadesh yisrael vehazemanim."

בָּרוּךְ אַתָּה יְיָ, מְקַדֵּשׁ יִשְׂרָאֵל וְהַזְּמַנִּים:

"Blessed are You, Lord our God, King of the Universe, who has given us life, kept us, and permitted us to be here today."

"Baruch Atah Adonay Eloheynu Melech haolam she-heche-yanu vek-iye-manu ve-hig-ianu lazeman hazeh."

בָּרוּךְ אַתָּה יְיָ, אֱלֹהֵינוּ מֶלֶךְ הָעוֹלָם, שֶׁהֶחֱיָנוּ וְקִיְּמָנוּ וְהִגִּיעָנוּ לַזְּמַן הַזֶּה:

Drink the Wine   *Uncover the matzah*

4

Washing
Your Hands

Wash your hands without saying the blessing.

We wash our hands as a symbol of being clean before we start the service.

Children help by bringing a water pitcher, a bowl and a towel around the table, so that family members can wash.

Parsley in Salt Water

Karpas

כַּרְפַּס

We dip this green vegetable into salt water and say the blessing:

"Blessed are You. Lord Our God, King of the Universe, who creates the fruit of the earth."

Baruch Atah Adonay Eloheynu Melech haolam borey peree ha-a-damah."

בָּרוּךְ אַתָּה יְיָ, אֱלֹהֵינוּ מֶלֶךְ הָעוֹלָם,
בּוֹרֵא פְּרִי הָאֲדָמָה:

Eat the Parsley.

When we eat the Parsley, it reminds us of the simple foods eaten as slaves and we are thankful that God gives us food that is grown in the ground. When we dip in salt water, we remember the tears of the sadness of slavery.

6

Making the Afikomen

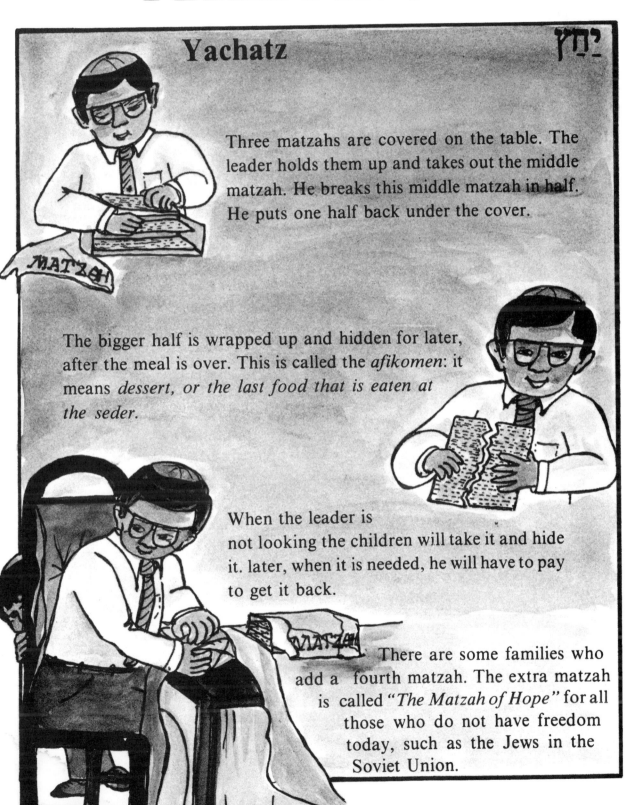

Yachatz

יַחַץ

Three matzahs are covered on the table. The leader holds them up and takes out the middle matzah. He breaks this middle matzah in half. He puts one half back under the cover.

The bigger half is wrapped up and hidden for later, after the meal is over. This is called the *afikomen*: it means *dessert, or the last food that is eaten at the seder.*

When the leader is not looking the children will take it and hide it. later, when it is needed, he will have to pay to get it back.

There are some families who add a fourth matzah. The extra matzah is called *"The Matzah of Hope"* for all those who do not have freedom today, such as the Jews in the Soviet Union.

Telling
the Story

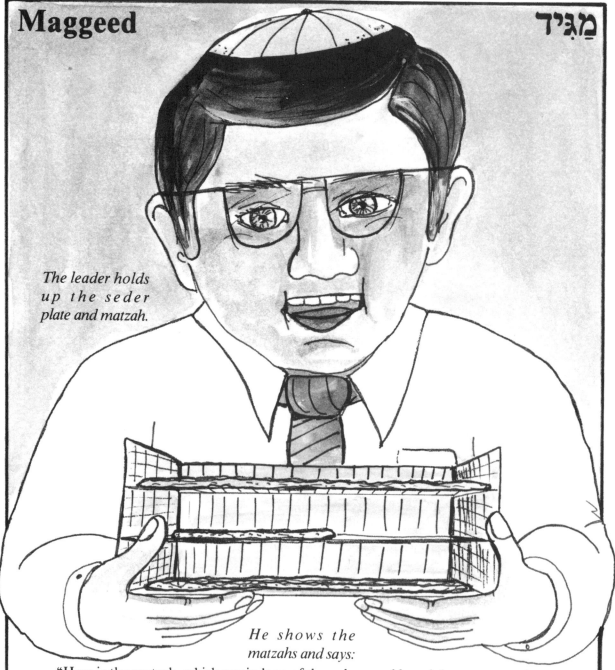

The leader holds up the seder plate and matzah.

He shows the matzahs and says:

"Here is the matzah, which reminds us of the unleavened bread that was eaten by our ancestors who were slaves in Egypt.

Anyone who is hungry may share what we have.

Anyone who does not have a Passover seder to go to may come and join our seder.

Tonight, we are here, next year may we be in the land of Israel.

Tonight, there are still Jews who are slaves, next year may they all be free."

The leader puts down the covered matzahs.   *The wine cups are filled for the second time.*

Asking the Four Questions

Why is this night of Passover different from all other nights of the year?

On all other nights, we eat either Chometz or Matzah, but on this night we eat only Matzah.

On all other nights, we eat all kinds of herbs, but on this night we eat only maror.

On all other nights, we do not dip even once, but on this night we dip twice.

On all other nights, we eat either sitting or reclining, but on this night we eat reclining.

Mah neesh-ta-nah ha-lai-loh ha-zeh mee-kal ha-lay-lot she-b'chal ha-lay lot a-noo och-leen chamaytz u-matzah ha-lay-lah ha-zeh kulo matzah
She-b'chal ha-lay-lot a-noo och-leen sh'ar y'ro-kot, ha-lai-loh ha-zeh ma-ror
She-b'chal ha-lay-lot ayn a-noo mat-bee-leen a-fee-loo pa-am e-chat, ha-lai-lah ha-zeh sh'tay f'ameem
She-b'chal ha-lay-lot a-noo och-leen bayn yosh-veen u-vayn m'su-been, ha-lai-lah ha-zeh ku-la-noo m'su-been.

מַה נִּשְׁתַּנָּה הַלַּיְלָה הַזֶּה מִכָּל הַלֵּילוֹת . שֶׁבְּכָל הַלֵּילוֹת אָנוּ אוֹכְלִין חָמֵץ וּמַצָּה . הַלַּיְלָה הַזֶּה כֻּלּוֹ מַצָּה : שֶׁבְּכָל הַלֵּילוֹת אָנוּ אוֹכְלִין שְׁאָר יְרָקוֹת. הַלַּיְלָה הַזֶּה מָרוֹר: שֶׁבְּכָל הַלֵּילוֹת אֵין אָנוּ מַטְבִּילִין אֲפִילוּ פַּעַם אֶחָת . הַלַּיְלָה הַזֶּה שְׁתֵּי פְעָמִים : שֶׁבְּכָל הַלֵּילוֹת אָנוּ אוֹכְלִין בֵּין יוֹשְׁבִין וּבֵין מְסֻבִּין. הַלַּיְלָה הַזֶּה כֻּלָּנוּ מְסֻבִּין :

Answers to The Questions

MATZAH

We eat matzah to remember the flat, hard bread that was made by the slaves as they ran from Egypt.

EGYPT
FREEDOM

MAROR

We eat maror tonight to remember how hard and bitter it was to be a slave.

Uncover the Matzah.

We were once slaves to Pharaoh in Egypt. God took us out of Egypt and saved us. If He did not save us, we might still be slaves in Egypt. We are no longer slaves, so today we tell the story of Passover. It is our job to tell the Passover story, and to do things to remember what happened to the Jewish people so many years ago.

DIPPING *We dip two times tonight.*

1) Parsley in salt water to change tears to thankfulness. The parsley is the fresh food of spring that we are happy to grow. The salt water is the tears of slavery.

2) Maror in charoses to sweeten bitterness and suffering. Charoses is made from chopped apples, nuts and wine. It is sweet, but it also looks like the cement that the slaves used to build Pharaoh's palaces.

RECLINING

Years ago, only free men could recline, or lean back in comfort when eating. Tonight we show that we are free, by reclining during the seder.

THE FOUR

We bless God
who gave us the Torah

When we tell the Passover story, we must make sure that everyone can understand it. We are told in the Torah about four different types of sons, or daughters, to whom we tell the story of Passover.

The Wise Son:

The wise son asks all about the Passover story and the rules that God gave us.
We teach him everything there is to know.

The Selfish Son:

The selfish son says that he does not want to know anything. He does not care what happened to the Jews in Egypt. After all, he was not there, so why should he do anything today?

We tell him that we do these things because *we* feel that *we* were taken out of slavery, and God would have saved us. But, since he feels the way he does, God would not have saved him if he were a slave years ago in Egypt.

SONS . . . . .

The Son who does not know how to ask:

This son asks us "what is happening here?"

We tell him that God did wonderful things for us when he took us out of Egypt and saved us from slavery. That is why it is important to remember and follow the laws.

The Son who is too young to ask:

It is our job to tell the full story of Passover to the little son who is too young to ask us. We tell him it is because of what God did for *us* when he took *us* out of Egypt. Therefore, we tell the entire story to all the little children tonight.

The Story of PASSOVER

Cover the Matzah and hold up the cup of wine.

GOD'S PROMISE

God always does what He promises. He told us that we would be slaves in a place that was not our true home, and that he would save us. God did save us. There have been other times that the Jewish people have been hurt, but God always helps us. Today, once again, Israel is the Jewish homeland that God promised. Whatever dangers Israel faces, God promises always to help us. And we believe in Him.

Put down the wine cup.

In the beginning, people prayed to idols. When Abraham was a boy, he believed in God and not the silly idols that his father made. God brought Abraham to the land of Canaan. He made a promise to Abraham that he would have children and they would become a great nation.

Abraham and his wife Sarah had a son named Isaac. Isaac had two sons named Jacob and Essau. Jacob had twelve sons. One son, Joseph, was in Egypt when Pharaoh had bad dreams. Joseph told him what the dreams meant, and Pharaoh liked him. Joseph helped the Pharaoh make sure that there would be plenty of food for all the people in Egypt. Pharaoh made Joseph a very important person in Egypt.

Meanwhile,

back in Canaan, there was no food to eat. So Joseph's father, Jacob, decided to take his family to Egypt, where there was plenty of food. When they got there, Pharaoh welcomed them since they were Joseph's family.

Jacob and his family did not plan to stay for a long time. But it turned out that they did.

The Jewish people became important and powerful. The Egyptians did not like this.

Then the good Pharaoh died, and a new mean Pharaoh became the ruler.

This new Pharaoh was afraid that if the Jews got too strong, they would take over Egypt. So, Pharaoh tricked them into slavery. The Jewish people were forced to do all kinds of hard and bitter work for the mean Pharaoh in Egypt.

Still, the Egyptians were afraid of the Jewish slaves, since there were so many of them. The Egyptians thought that in a war the Jewish slaves might become too strong and join with the Egyptian's enemies to fight against them.

Pharaoh then ordered that all baby boys born to the Jewish slaves be killed. This way, the slaves would not have any strong men.

The Jewish people cried to God to save them — God did hear them.

To save her new-born son, one mother put her baby in a basket. She told her daughter, Miriam, to hide him in the river. Miriam put the basket in the river. Then she hid in the bushes to watch what happened.

After a while, Pharaoh's daughter came to the river to bathe. She found the basket with the little baby boy inside. The Princess decided that she wanted to keep the baby and she took him home to Pharaoh's palace. She called the baby "Moses", which means "taken out of the water."

The Princess needed a nurse for Moses. Miriam brought a nurse to the Princess. The nurse was Moses' real mother. She secretly raised him as a Jew, and that stayed with him even as he grew up in the Pharaoh's palace.

The Princess called Moses her son, and he had all the privileges of a Prince of Egypt.

While he was growing up, he saw a lot of bad treatment of the slaves. He did not like it.

Then, one day, he saw a Jewish slave being badly beaten by an Egyptian.

When he went to stop the beating, he ended up killing the cruel Egyptian.

Moses was now in trouble. He knew that Pharaoh would punish him, so he ran away from Egypt.

Moses became a shepard in a land far-away from Egypt. He married and had children and lived there many years.

One day when Moses was out in the fields with his sheep, he saw a burning bush. Moses went closer to the bush. It was on fire, but nothing was being burned up. Then a voice came out of the flames on the bush. It was God's voice talking to Moses.

God told Moses to go back to Egypt and free the Jewish slaves. Moses had to save them from the mean Pharaoh. Moses did not believe that he could accomplish this great task, but he obeyed God's words.

19

Moses went back to Egypt and told the mean Pharaoh to let the slaves go free. But, Pharaoh would not listen.

"**NO!** I will not let them go!" he said.

No matter what Moses said or did, Pharaoh still said no. So, God had to send plagues to make him change his mind. After each plague, Pharaoh changed his mind and would not let the slaves go.

God sent ten plagues before Pharaoh let the slaves go.

The Ten Plagues

Each time we say the name of one of the Plagues, we take a drop of wine out of our wine cups. We can use toothpicks, and place the drop of wine on paper napkins or our plates.

A full cup of wine means happiness. When we name the plagues and take wine from the cup, we are remembering the unhappiness that others felt.

Blood - דָּם
Dam

Frogs - צְפַרְדֵּעַ
Tzefardeya

We do not drink the drops of wine that stand for the plagues and unhappiness

21

'Lice - כִּנִּים
Keeneem

Wild Beasts - עָרוֹב
Arov

22

Sickness of Cattle - דֶּבֶר
Dever

Boils - שְׁחִין
Shocheen

Hail - בָּרָד
Barad

Locusts - אַרְבֶּה
Arbeh

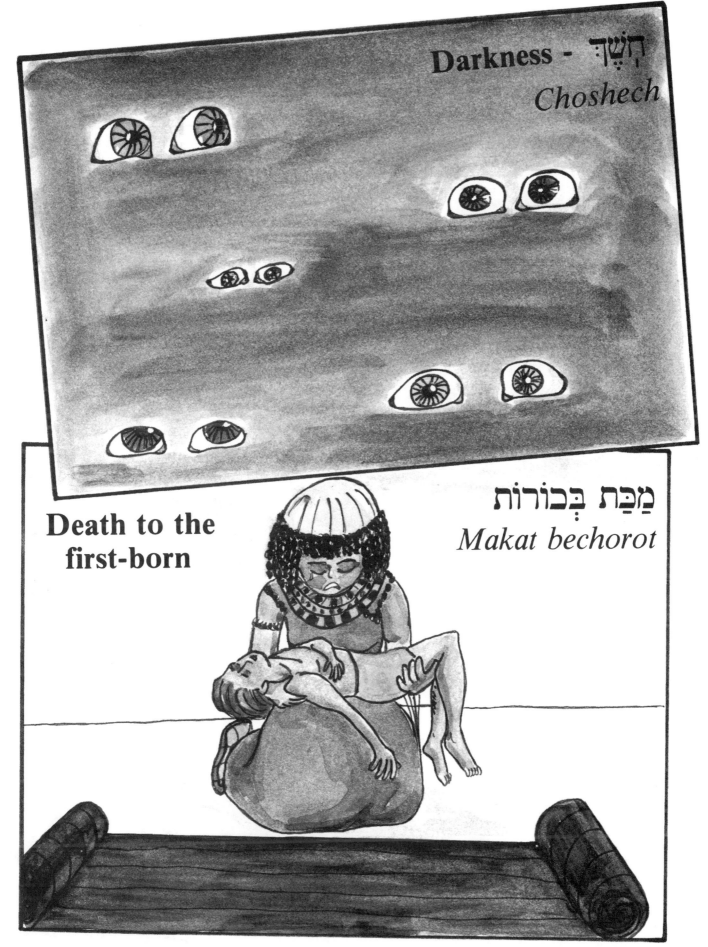

Darkness - חֹשֶׁךְ
Choshech

Death to the
first-born

מַכַּת בְּכוֹרוֹת
Makat bechorot

After God sent the tenth plague, and Pharaoh's son died, Pharaoh told Moses to take all the slaves and leave Egypt! God took the Jews out of slavery and out of Egypt!

The people quickly gathered together. They took their belongings and many of the riches of Egypt. God led Moses and the Jewish people out of Egypt and into the dessert.

They went quickly, because they did not trust Pharaoh. They were afraid that when Pharaoh realized that all the slaves were gone, he would try to bring them back. They did not have time to wait for the dough to rise for the bread that they needed. So, they baked the flat dough in the sun as they traveled — and they ate matzah.

Sure enough, mean Pharaoh did change his mind. He sent his army after the Jews, telling the soldiers to bring them all back to him.

The Jews were at the Red Sea bank when they saw the soldiers coming after them.

"We are trapped!" they cried. "The soldiers are behind us and the Red Sea is in front of us. God help us!"

At that moment, God divided the water of the Red Sea, making a pathway. All the people walked across on dry land. When everyone was on the otherside of the sea, God closed the waters. All the soldiers who were chasing them were drowned. Pharaoh's army was gone, and the Jewish people were free!

SING THE SONG

Let's sing about all the wonderful things that God did for us.

1. God took us out of Egypt.

 **2.** God punished the Egyptians.

3. God destroyed all their idols.

 **4.** God killed the first-born Egyptians.

5. God gave us the riches of Egypt.

  **6.** God divided the Red Sea for us.

7. God let us cross the sea on dry land.

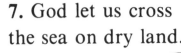  **8.** God drowned the Egyptian army.

28

DAYANU

9. God took care of us in the desert where we lived for forty (40) years.

10. God fed us with manna from heaven.

11. God gave us the Shabbath, our day of rest.

12. God brought us to Mount Sinai.

13. God gave us the Torah and Ten Commandments.

14. God led us to the promised land of Israel.

15. God built the Holy Temple for us.

If God had done only one of these things, it would have been enough. We would not have asked for more. But, God did do all these things for us. We are thankful for everything that He did. We sing this song Dayanu which means, "it would have been enough."

THE SYMBOLS

To tell the full Passover story, we must say three things out loud. They are: Pesach (Passover), Matzah, and Maror.

The shank bone on the seder plate is a symbol of the Passover Lamb that was eaten when we had the Temple to pray in. It is a symbol of the lamb's blood that was put over the doors of the Jewish homes the night of the tenth plague in Egypt. We remember that God 'passed over' the homes of our people when He killed the first-born Egyptians.

PESACH (PASSOVER) פֶּסַח

OF PASSOVER

MATZAH

The matzah is the flat bread that the Jews ate when they ran from Egypt. They did not have time to wait and let the dough rise. They made matzah. We eat this matzah to remember.

מַצָּה

MAROR

Maror is the bitter herbs, or vegetables, that we eat tonight. We eat them to remember how hard, or bitter, the lives of the Jews were made when we were slaves to Pharaoh in Egypt.

מָרוֹר

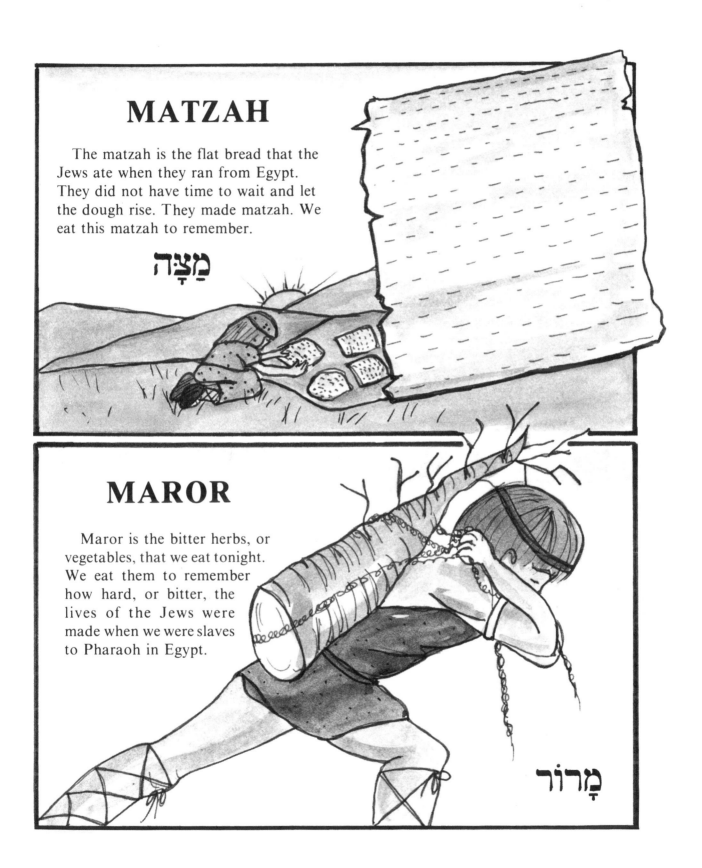

We Were Saved

We all must pretend that we, ourselves, are being freed.
It is important to feel that God saved us, you and me,
and our families from being slaves in Egypt
and brought us to the promised land
of Israel.

Cover the Matzo.
Hold up the cup of wine and say:

We must say Thank You to God for all the things that he has done for us. We must sing a song of thanks to Him. He took us from slavery to freedom, from sadness to happiness, from pain to joy, and from darkness to light. Now we sing the song Halleluyah!

Put down the cup of wine.

Halleluyah

Halleluyah, Praise the servants of the Lord,
Praise the Name of the Lord

From morning to night
Praise the Lord's Name

The Lord is above all nations
His glory is above the heavens

Who is like our God, who is so high
Who looks down on heaven and earth

Who lifts up the poorest and neediest person
To sit with princes of his people

He makes the childless woman
a happy mother of children, Halleluyah!

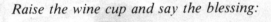

Raise the wine cup and say the blessing:

"Blessed are You, Lord our God, King of the Universe, who has taken us out of slavery in Egypt, and permitted us to be here tonight to eat the matzah and maror. May we be able to live in peace and celebrate many more holidays. May we be able to live in Israel and rebuild the Holy Temple so we can thank You again for our freedom with a new song."

"Blessed are You, Lord our God, who has given us back a free Israel."

"Blessed are You, Lord our God, King of the Universe, who creates the fruit of the vine."

"Baruch Atah Adonay Eloheynu Melech haolam boray peree hagafen."

בָּרוּךְ אַתָּה יְיָ, אֱלֹהֵינוּ מֶלֶךְ הָעוֹלָם, בּוֹרֵא פְּרִי הַגָּפֶן:

Drink the second cup of wine.

33

Rachatz
Washing Your Hands

We wash our hands as we get ready to eat the Passover Meal. The children bring around the water pitcher, bowl and towel for everyone to use. This time, we say the blessing.

"Blessed are You, Lord our God, King of the Universe, who has given us your commandments and tells us to wash our hands.

"*Baruch Atah Adonay Eloheynu Melech haolam a-sher keedeshanu bemeetz-vo-sav v-tzee-vanu al ne-tee-las yadayeem*"

בָּרוּךְ אַתָּה יְיָ אֱלֹהֵינוּ מֶלֶךְ הָעוֹלָם, אֲשֶׁר קִדְּשָׁנוּ בְּמִצְוֹתָיו, וְצִוָּנוּ עַל נְטִילַת יָדָיִם:

Motzee Matzah
Eating the Matzah

מוֹצִיא מַצָּה

We break up the matzah on the matzah plate and give everyone a piece. First we say these two blessings:

"Blessed are You, Lord our God, King of the Universe, who brings forth bread from the earth."

"*Baruch Atah Adonay Eloheynu Melech haolam hamotzee lechem meen ha-aretz.*"

בָּרוּךְ אַתָּה יְיָ, אֱלֹהֵינוּ מֶלֶךְ הָעוֹלָם, הַמּוֹצִיא לֶחֶם מִן הָאָרֶץ:

"Blessed are You, Lord our God, King of the Universe, who has given us your commandments and told us to eat matzah."

"*Baruch Atah Adonay Eloheynu Melech haolam asher keedshanu b-meetz-vo-tav v-tzee-vanu al acheelat matzah*"

בָּרוּךְ אַתָּה יְיָ, אֱלֹהֵינוּ מֶלֶךְ הָעוֹלָם, אֲשֶׁר קִדְּשָׁנוּ בְּמִצְוֹתָיו וְצִוָּנוּ עַל אֲכִילַת מַצָּה:

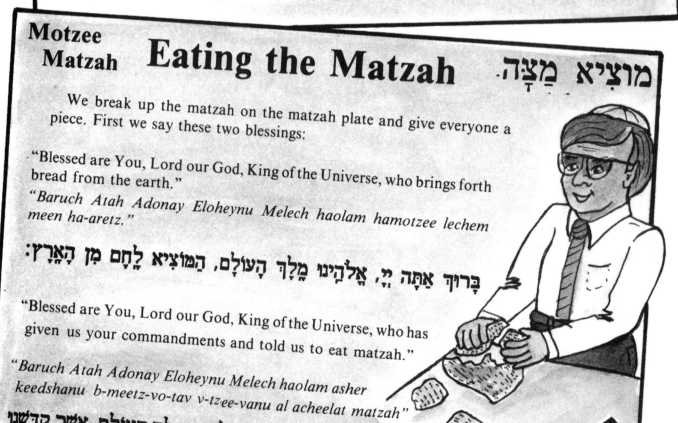

Now we eat the matzah.

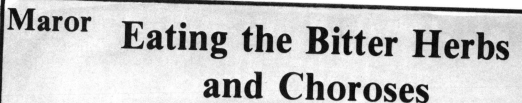

Maror

Eating the Bitter Herbs and Choroses

מָרוֹר

Mix a piece of the maror — the bitter herb, or horseradish — with some of the sweet choroses. The choroses looks like the mortar that was used to glue together the bricks that the slaves had to make. When we eat this we remember the bitterness of slavery, and the sweetness of God saving us.

Say the Blessing:

"Blessed are You, Lord our God, King of the Universe, who has given us your commandments and told us to eat the bitter herbs."

"Baruch Atah Adonay Eloheynu Melech haolam asher keedshanu b-meetz-vo-tav v-tzee-vanu al acheelat maror."

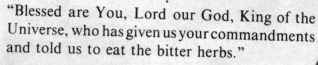

בָּרוּךְ אַתָּה יְיָ אֱלֹהֵינוּ מֶלֶךְ הָעוֹלָם, אֲשֶׁר קִדְּשָׁנוּ בְּמִצְוֹתָיו וְצִוָּנוּ עַל אֲכִילַת מְרוֹר

Eat the maror and choroses.

Matzah and Maror Sandwich

Koraych

כּוֹרֵךְ

We put a piece of the maror between two small pieces of matzah and say this:

"When remembering the Holy Temple, we do what the wise Hillel did at that time. He put the matzah and the bitter herbs together so he could do what the Torah says: Eat the Passover Lamb with matzah and bitter herbs.

Eat the sandwich.

Eating the Festive

We enjoy the festive Passover meal with our family. It is a big meal with many dishes. What is your holiday meal like? This is what a lot families like to eat:

We start the meal by eating hard boiled eggs with salt water. The egg has many meanings.

1. One is a symbol of the holiday offering at the time of the Temple.

2. Some people believe the egg we eat is a symbol of springtime and new life.

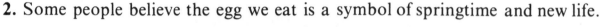

3. The hard boiled egg is said to be like the Jewish people. The egg is good no matter how hard it is cooked in boiling water, and the Jewish people will survive no matter how much trouble they have.

4. The egg in salt water also reminds us of the Jews crossing the Red Sea.

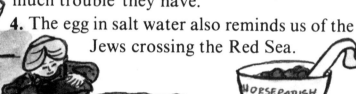

Next comes a delicious piece of gefilite fish, with a slice of cooked carrot on top, Yum!

Then we have chicken soup with matzah balls.

Passover Meal . . . .

Shulchan Aruch

שֻׁלְחָן עוֹרֵךְ

We should recline and eat slowly to show that we are free. The main course is yet to come. Maybe it is a delicious turkey with all the trimmings, or a juicy roast. Whatever we eat, we get to enjoy the meal with our family and friends. No one can rush us, and we are free to enjoy ourselves.

Now, finished with the meal, we save space for the dessert — the afikomen.

The Afikomen

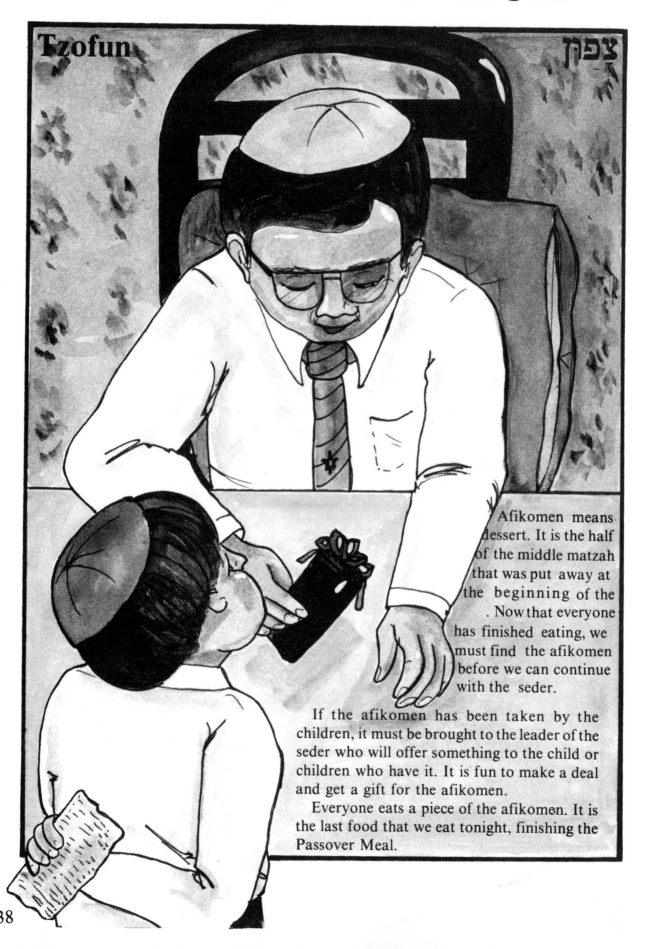

Tzofun   צפן

Afikomen means dessert. It is the half of the middle matzah that was put away at the beginning of the . Now that everyone has finished eating, we must find the afikomen before we can continue with the seder.

If the afikomen has been taken by the children, it must be brought to the leader of the seder who will offer something to the child or children who have it. It is fun to make a deal and get a gift for the afikomen.

Everyone eats a piece of the afikomen. It is the last food that we eat tonight, finishing the Passover Meal.

Grace After the Meal

Baraych

בָּרֵךְ

Pour the third cup of wine, then we say grace

"Let us Bless God's name forever and ever."

"Yehee shaym Adonay m-vo-rach mayatah v-ad olam."

יְהִי שֵׁם יְיָ מְבֹרָךְ מֵעַתָּה וְעַד עוֹלָם.

"Blessed is He who gave us the food we ate and is good to us in our lives."

"Blessed are You, Lord our God, King of the Universe, who feeds the entire world and takes care of all creatures. With goodness and kindness we always have and will have food. You take care of all our needs.

Raise the cup of wine.

We are going to drink this cup of wine in thankfulness for the freedom that God gave to our fathers who were slaves in Egypt. We are thankful for all the food from the earth that we have eaten.

Say the blessing.

"Blessed are You, Lord our God, King of the Universe, who creates the fruit of the vine."

"Baruch Atah Adonay Eloheynu Melech haolam boray peree hagafen."

בָּרוּךְ אַתָּה יְיָ, אֱלֹהֵינוּ מֶלֶךְ הָעוֹלָם,
בּוֹרֵא פְּרִי הַגָּפֶן:

Drink the wine.

39

Wine for Elijah the Prophet

We put a special cup of wine on the table for Elijah the Prophet. Elijah was a wise teacher who lived many years ago. There is a legend that he visits every Jewish home on the night of the seder, and wishes everyone a year full of freedom and peace.

We open the door to show that we want to welcome him into our seder. After we close the door, we look to see if he drank any of the wine in his cup that we put on the table.

Songs of Praise

Hallel   *Fill the fourth cup of wine.*   הַלֵּל

We sing songs of praise to God, of all His people and His good deeds. We praise him for His great kindness and truth forever.

Say Halleluyah.

We thank God because He is good, His kindness lasts forever. Let all Israel say His kindness lasts forever. Let the people of Aaron say His kindness lasts forever. Let all those who worship the Lord say that His kindness lasts forever.

We give thanks to Him for all that He does and all that He is.

41

The Fourth Cup of Wine

Hold up the fourth cup of wine.

Say the Blessing:

"Blessed are You, Lord our God, King of the Universe who creates the fruit of the vine."

בָּרוּךְ אַתָּה יְיָ, אֱלֹהֵינוּ
מֶלֶךְ הָעוֹלָם, בּוֹרֵא פְּרִי הַגָּפֶן:

"Baruch Atah Adonay Eloheynu Melech haolam boray peree hagafen."

Drink the wine.

Closing Prayer

Nirtzah

נִרְצָה:

The seder is finished. We have heard the story of Passover. We have eaten all the special foods and mentioned all the symbols of the holiday.

This year we are happy to celebrate Passover in freedom.

Next year we hope to again be able to enjoy the seder as free people. We hope that Israel will stay a strong and free country for all Jewish people.

And we say:

NEXT YEAR IN JERUSALEM!

"L-shanah haba-ah b-yerushalayeem."

לְשָׁנָה הַבָּאָה בִּירוּשָׁלַיִם:

Who Knows One ?

A Song to Sing after the seder. Each time you sing a new number, add all the numbers before it, until you get to one. At the end you will have a long list to sing. Have fun.

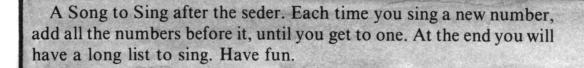

1. Who knows one? I know one.
One is for our God in heaven
and on earth.

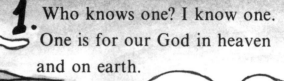

2. Who know two? I know two.
Two is for the tablets God gave
to us on Mount Sinai.

Who knows three. I know three.
3. Three is for the fathers of our people.

Who knows four? I know four. **4.** Four is for the mothers
of our nation,

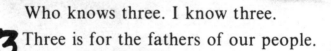

5. Who knows five. I know five.
Five is for the books of the Torah,

6. Who knows six? I know six.
Six is for the parts of the Mishnah.

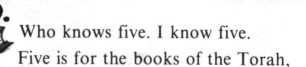

7. Who knows seven? I know seven.
Seven is for the days of the week,

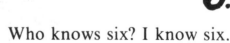

ECHOD MEE YODAYA
אֶחָד מִי יוֹדֵעַ

Who knows eight? I know eight.
Eight is for the days before the Brith, **8.**

Who knows nine? I know nine.
Nine is for the months for a baby to be born. **9**

Who knows ten? I know ten.
Ten is for the ten commandments, **10.**

Who knows eleven? I know eleven.
Eleven is for the stars in **11.** Joseph's dream,

Who knows twelve? I know twelve.
Twelve is for the tribes of Israel. **12.**

Who knows thirteen? I know thirteen.
13. Thirteen is for the wonderful ways of God,

Twelve is for the tribes of Israel;
Eleven is for the stars in Joseph's dream;
Ten is for the ten commandments; Nine is for the months for a baby to be born;
Eight is for the days before Brith; Seven is for the days of the week;
Six is for the parts of the Mishnah; Five is for the books of the Torah;
Four is for the mothers of our nation; Three is for the fathers of our people;
Two is for the tablets God gave to us on Mount Sinai;
One is for our God in heaven and on earth.

CHAD GADYA חַד גַּדְיָא,

This song reminds us about the history of the Jewish people. Everything seems to try and destroy the Jews, but God will not let it happen. In the end we will survive. The two zuzim (coins) represent the tablets of the ten commandments which our father (God) gave for the goat (the Jewish people).

Just like in WHO KNOWS ONE, each time you sing another phrase, you add all the others to it. Repeat the chorus after each phrase.

Chorus: One little goat, one little goat.

One little goat, one little goat, that my father bought for two zuzim

chorus

Then along came a cat and ate the goat that my father bought for two zuzim
chorus

Then came a stick that beat the dog,

Then came a dog that bit the cat,

Then came a fire that burnt the stick,

Then came the water that put out the fire,

46

ONE GOAT חַד גַּדְיָא,

Then came the ox that drank the water,

Then came the butcher
who killed the ox,

Then came the angel of death
that killed the butcher,

Then came the Holy One, Blessed be He,

who killed the angel of death,
who killed the butcher,
who killed the ox,
who drank the water,
that put out the fire,
that burnt the stick,
that beat the dog,
that bit the cat,
that ate the goat,
that my father bought for two zuzim.

Chorus: One little goat, One little goat.

It's Passover Time

words and music by Linda Tsuruoka

Set the ta - ble pour out the wine Se - der's here it's

Pass - o - ver time Tell the an - cient sto - ry once more

that is what the Se - der is for Set a place for E - li - ya - hu

ask four ques - tions sing Da - ye - nu hide the ma - tza

dip in the wine Se - der's here it's Pass - o - ver time

Reprinted with the permission of the composer from the book COLOR 'N' SING by Jacqueline Pliskin and Linda Tsuruoka, Tara publications.